P9-DMU-461

Dear Imagination Library Graduate,

My, how time flies. It seems it was only yesterday when your family and friends read you your first story. You were just a baby. Now you're five years old and about to go to school. How exciting!

This may be your last book from my Imagination Library but you have to promise me you will keep on reading. If you go to your local public library you will find a great number of books just for kids your age. Every book is a treasure and every time you open one up you will meet new friends and take wonderful journeys to magical places.

I hope you have a great time in school. I bet your school will even have a library where you can check out books. You and all of your friends are very special. There is no limit to what you can do or how far you can go. Just remember the lessons my family taught me – dream big dreams; learn everything you can learn; and care for all those who care for you. You do all of these things and you can be anyone you want to be.

You are terrific, and remember . . .

I Will Always Love You,

Dolly

Look Out
Kindergarten,
Here I Come!

by Nancy Carlson

VIKING

VIKING
Published by the Penguin Group
Penguin Putnam Books for Young Readers, 345 Hudson Street, New York, New York 10014, U.S.A.
Penguin Books Ltd, 27 Wrights Lane, London W8 5TZ, England
Penguin Books Australia Ltd, Ringwood, Victoria, Australia
Penguin Books Canada Ltd, 10 Alcorn Avenue, Toronto, Ontario, Canada M4V 3B2
Penguin Books (N.Z.) Ltd, 182-190 Wairau Road, Auckland 10, New Zealand

Penguin Books Ltd, Registered Offices: Harmondsworth, Middlesex, England

First published in 1999 by Viking, a member of Penguin Putnam Books for Young Readers.

28 29 30 31 32

Copyright © Nancy Carlson, 1999
All rights reserved

LIBRARY OF CONGRESS CATALOGING-IN-PUBLICATION DATA
Carlson, Nancy L.
Look out, kindergarten, here I come! / Nancy Carlson.
p. cm.
Summary: Even though Henry is looking forward to going to
kindergarten, he is not sure about staying once he first gets there.

ISBN: 0-670-03597-1
Special Markets ISBN 978-0-670-03597-7 Not for Resale

[1. Kindergarten—Fiction. 2. First day of school—Fiction.]
I. Title.
PZ7.C21665Lim 1999 [E]—dc21 98-47039 CIP AC

Manufactured in China
Set in Avenir

Without limiting the rights under copyright reserved above, no part of this publication may be reproduced, stored in or intro-
duced into a retrieval system, or transmitted, in any form or by any means (electronic, mechanical, photocopying, recording or
otherwise), without the prior written permission of both the copyright owner and the above publisher of this book.

This Imagination Library edition is published by Penguin Young Readers, a division
of Penguin Random House, exclusively for Dolly Parton's Imagination Library,
a not-for-profit program designed to inspire a love of reading and learning, sponsored
in part by The Dollywood Foundation. Penguin's trade editions of this work are
available wherever books are sold.

To Maureen Beck—a dedicated educator who helped
me come up with the idea for this book

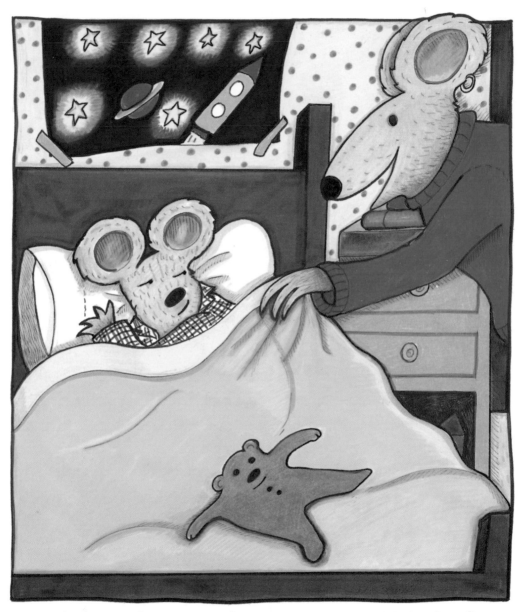

"Wake up, dear," said Henry's mom. "It's the first day of kindergarten."

"Oh boy! Let's go!" said Henry. He had been
getting ready for this day all year.
"Not so fast," said his mom. "First you need to
wash up and get dressed."

So Henry brushed his teeth the way his dentist had shown him and washed behind his ears.

Then he buttoned his shirt and snapped his jeans
and *almost* tied his shoes.

"Okay, I'm all ready for kindergarten!" said Henry.
"Not so fast," said his mom. "First you need a
good breakfast."

So Henry ate three  pancakes and a bowl
of fruit and drank a big glass of milk.

"Now I'm ready to go!" said Henry.
"Not so fast," said his mom. "You still need to pack up your supplies."

So Henry packed pencils, scissors, crayons, paper, glue, an apple, and . . .

a photo of his mom and dad
(in case he got lonely).

"Now I'm ready!"
said Henry.

"What do you think we'll do first?" asked Henry.
"Do you think we'll paint?"

"Sure you will," said his mom. "Just like at home."
"Good!" said Henry. "What else will we do?"

"You'll probably learn your ABCs," said his mom.

"Hey, I already know the letters in my name!" said
Henry. "What will we do after that?"

"You'll sing songs,

and play games,

and you might practice counting," said his mom.

"One, two, three flowers," said Henry. "I can count to ten, because we practiced counting with buttons. What comes next?"

"You'll make fun things in arts and crafts, and you'll read stories."

"But I can't read!" said Henry.
"That's okay," said his mom. "You'll start by listening. Reading comes later."

"Here we are," said Henry's mom.
"It's so *big*," said Henry. "What if I get lost?"

"Remember, we found your room and your
cubby at Kindergarten Roundup," said his mom.
"But you can always ask a teacher for help."

When Henry got to his room and
saw lots of new faces, he said,

"I want to go home!"

"Why don't you come in and look around?" said his teacher, Ms. Bradley.

So Henry looked around. He saw the art corner.
He saw letters and numbers that he knew.

He saw a bookcase full of books, and he met a new friend to play with.

"Well, what do you think?" asked Henry's mom.
"I think I might stay for a while, Mom," said Henry,

"because kindergarten is going to be fun!"